A BAN

THE
GOLDEN BIRD

Berlie Doherty

Illustrated by
JOHN LAWRENCE

HEINEMANN·LONDON

For Andrew, Rob and Peter
- and all the New Vic crew

William Heinemann Ltd
an imprint of Reed Consumer Books Ltd
Michelin House
81 Fulham Road London SW3 6RB
Auckland · Melbourne · Singapore · Toronto

First published 1995
Reprinted 1996
Text copyright © 1995 Berlie Doherty
Illustrations copyright © 1995 John Lawrence
ISBN 0 434 96799 8

Printed in Italy by Olivotto

A school pack of BANANA BOOKS 73-78 is
available from Heinemann Educational Books
ISBN 0 434 97224 X

One

'BY THE WAY,' said Mr Swain as his class was clearing up at the end of the afternoon. 'I've finished writing the school play.'

He had everyone's immediate attention. Only Andrew kept his head down.

'It's based on the story of the Sleeping Beauty,' Mr Swain went on.

Lynne beamed round at everyone, then closed her eyes.

'And I've cast it,' said Mr Swain. 'Eddie is to be the king.'

Eddie heaved a sigh of relief and grinned at Craig. He waved his hand in a lordly fashion. He would be regal and mighty. He would shout out his lines and make his courtiers quiver. The audience would quiver. Everyone would be afraid of him.

Craig sniffed. He was bored already. He wanted to be out in the playground, kicking his football around.

'Sarah is queen.' Sarah blushed and put her hands over her face. Under their cover she smiled to herself. She would wear a sparkly crown and flashing jewellery, and a wonderful flowing silver dress. Everybody would say how beautiful she was. Lynne opened her eyes and poked her.

'Richard is the cook.'

'Cook!' Richard was alarmed. 'That's a girl's part.'

'Shows how much you know,' said Lynne. 'All the cooks in the posh hotels are men. They wear floppy hats and . . .'

'And strings of sausages round their necks,' said Mr Swain. 'You'll be a very good cook, Richard. It's an important character part. Nearly the main part.'

'Who's Sleeping Beauty?' Lynne demanded. 'That's the main part.'

'Georgina,' said Mr Swain.

Georgina stared at him.

'Georgina!' shouted Lynne. 'GeorgINA?'

'She's only been here a week,' grumbled Shaz.

'And she's not exactly beautiful, either,' said Lynne. 'Not what I call beautiful.'

'Georgina has a lovely singing voice,' said Mr Swain. 'And that's one of the reasons why I've given her the part.'

If Georgina had had the courage, she would have run up to the front of the classroom and given Mr Swain a hug. Yesterday at break-time he had talked to her and she had told him that one day she wanted to be a famous singer and then he had asked her to sing her favourite song to him. She had been so nervous then that her voice had come out in little broken trickles, full of fog and tremble, but he hadn't seemed to notice.

'And the prince is Craig.'
Scarlet-faced, Craig put his head down and his hands over his ears.

'You have to kiss her! You have to kiss Georgina!' Eddie crowed. 'I wouldn't be the prince for ANYthing!'

Everyone laughed, even Lynne. 'I'm glad I'm not Sleeping Beauty,' she said. 'Craig's always dribbling. Fancy being kissed by CRAIG! Yuk!'

'The fairies are . . .'

The teacher's voice was drowned in laughter as the boys turned round and jeered at the girls.

'QUIET! The fairies are Peter, Tim, Howard, Steve, Chad, Rob . . .'

At the back of the classroom
Andrew sat and stared out of the
window. He let the laughter and jeers
wash over him. It was always like this,
since the day he had stopped being
happy. He couldn't talk properly any
more. He went to a special teacher
once a week and even she was in
despair over him.

He stammered and stuttered, his teeth stuck together and his jaw jammed shut. And everyone laughed at him.

It was easier if he didn't talk at all. At least when he didn't talk people stopped noticing him. If they didn't notice him they didn't laugh at him. He liked it better that way. He pretended he was a ghost, and that nobody knew he was there. He just wished the afternoon bell would go and he could get away and go home.

'But the fairies are BOYS!' spluttered Lynne. 'That's stupid!'

'Except for the wicked fairy,' smiled Mr Swain. 'And that's you.'

Two

AT LAST THE bell went. The class rushed out in a flurry of laughing and joking. Everyone was excited at the thought of the school play, even though Mr Swain had some odd ideas about casting. That was because he was new, they decided. Mr Swain gave them all notes to their parents explaining that they would have to stay behind after school some evenings for rehearsals.

As always, Andrew waited until all the others had left before he stood up. Mr Swain was busy marking at the desk, and Andrew tiptoed up the aisle, careful not to touch any of the desks or chairs as he passed them, in case he made a noise. He had almost reached

the door when Mr Swain looked up
from his work.

'By the way, Andrew,' he said. 'I've
written in a part for you.'

Andrew stopped. He didn't look at
the teacher, but kept his eyes fixed on
the door handle. As soon as Mr Swain
finished speaking he would slip out
into the yard.

'I'd like you to play the part of the
golden bird.' Mr Swain looked up.
'If you'd like to, that is.'

Andrew said nothing.

'Think about it, Andrew.'

Rehearsals began the next day.
Mr Swain brought copies of the script
for everyone to look at.

'The play begins with a song,' he
said. 'And I want everyone to sing it
together. Have a go now, just saying
the words.'

Slowly the class began, all reciting
in a higgledy piggledy fashion, so the
words bumped into each other. But
Andrew just stared out of the window.

Birds were playing in the field, lifting
themselves up and away, swooping and
gliding, soaring up towards the clouds.

'Start again,' said Mr Swain.

'We will tell you a story
Of once upon a time,
Of a king and a queen who were
granted a wish,
Of a princess who slept for a
hundred years,
And a prince who woke her up with
a kiss;
Of a wicked fairy's evil curse,
And a golden bird with magic
powers . . .'

'Hang on!' Lynne interrupted the
chanting. 'You didn't tell us about the
golden bird. Who's she?'

Mr Swain looked round the
classroom at no one in particular.
'Do we have a golden bird?' he asked.

Andrew made himself turn away
from the window. He didn't dare trust
himself to speak. All he knew, with
every bone in his body, was that he
wanted to be the golden bird. He
nodded his head very slightly and then
looked away again.

'Yes, we do have a golden bird,' said Mr Swain. 'And I'll tell you all later who it is. Now. You did the chant quite well, in the end. Mr Palmer will be writing some music for it. First you'll all come on as jugglers and musicians – a really lively start to the play before it quietens into a magic story. Can anyone here juggle?'

Shaz put up her hand. 'My mum's learning circus skills at night-school. I can juggle, walk on stilts, spin plates, eat fire . . .'

'Juggling will do, Shaz. Pick two boys and two girls and you can teach them to juggle with these special juggling balls. NOTHING ELSE IS TO BE USED. I don't want anybody getting knocked out before the play even starts. The rest of you choose instruments. All the fairies can have bells round their ankles.'

Lynne pushed Tim and Howard over in her eagerness to get to the bells first.

'Except Lynne,' Mr Swain said.

She stood with her mouth wide open, staring at him in disbelief. 'That's not fair. That's just not fair!'

'I don't think it would do for the wicked fairy to have bells around her ankles. Just be satisfied with having the most exciting part in the play. Go away somewhere and practise a really wicked cackle, will you?'

Weeping, Lynne retreated to the end of the hall, snatching one of the juggling balls in mid-air as she passed.

Mr Swain gazed around him. It was bedlam. Yellow, red and green juggling balls were cascading round the room.

The jugglers were shouting and laughing at each other, squirming under their chairs and through legs.

Minstrels were shaking bells and banging drums and tambourines. A recorder group was practising scales. Lynne was laughing loudly and wickedly. The head-teacher peered round the door, waved, and backed out quickly.

Andrew was standing with his back to everyone. His chin rested on his hands, his elbows on the window ledge. He stared and stared at the movements of the birds in the yard outside.

He didn't move again until everyone had gone home. Mr Swain had gone off to the music cupboard to lock away all the instruments. Andrew turned away from the window. The birds had all flown well away from the shouting children, but he didn't need to watch them any more.

He started with his neck. He hunched his shoulders slightly so his head jutted forward. Now he practised moving his head. He jerked it from side to side in quick, light movements. He pretended his nose was a beak. He lifted his head and peered down his nose, pretending he could only see a tiny area each side of it. He cocked his head from side to side to look in other directions, always being careful to look straight down his beak.

Now he would concentrate on his wings. He stood up as straight as he could, with his shoulders still slightly hunched and his head to one side. His wings would sprout from his shoulder blades. He shrugged his shoulders to loosen them up and then spread out the feathers of his fingers. He flexed his shoulder muscles and gently rippled his arms up and down, like waves. His movements became slower and steadier and stronger. Then he lifted his head, opened his beak, and pretended to sing.

Three

THERE WAS A roar of excitement from
the class on the day that Mr Swain and
Miss Evans brought in the costumes.
Some of them hung loosely from coat
hangers and others were piled up in a
big wicker basket. All the children had
to sit down and wait with their arms
folded until they were called to have
their costumes handed out to them.

'The fairies first,' smiled Miss Evans.
The six boy fairies all groaned, and
their friends jeered and whistled.
Lynne had told them that they would
be wearing white ballet dresses with
tinselly wings, and holding sticks with
silver stars on them for wands. One by
one Miss Evans drew from her basket
six wonderful sky coloured cloaks with

deep hoods. They had rivers and mountains and leaves and flowers sewn into them, and when the boys put them on, they flowed round them with every movement they made.

'Wonderful,' said Mr Swain. 'You really do look like magic people.'

'What about their wings?' Lynne demanded.

'No wings,' said Miss Evans. 'We've decided there's only going to be one character with wings, and that will be the golden bird.'

'Who is the golden bird?' Craig asked. Everyone looked round. Andrew stared in front of him.

'I think Mr Swain is going to do it!' Shaz giggled.

'The wicked fairy's costume is the same, but black,' said Miss Evans. Lynne was upset.

She had been practising ballet steps
all week at home. She couldn't possibly
do ballet steps in that long cloak
without falling over it. Mr Swain
draped the cloak round her and she
practised swirling across the room.

'Hiss!' everyone hissed.

She cackled hideously.

Miss Evans handed out the rest of
the costumes and the children were
allowed to walk round for a bit to get
used to them before the rehearsal
started. The fairies swept round the
room, with their cloaks flowing. Eddie
and Sarah tried to swirl their royal
cloaks and tripped over the hems. The
recorder players squeaked into giggles.

'Mine's too long!' Sarah moaned.
'Everybody's laughing at me.'

'And my crown's too big!' said
Eddie. 'I can't possibly frighten
everybody with my crown slipping
over my nose like this.'

'You'll make a wonderful comedy
act!' Mr Swain laughed. 'I'm fed up of
seeing stuffy kings and queens in
plays. You'll cheer everyone up, the
pair of you.'

Sarah flounced away in disgust and
tripped over her cloak again. She
looked round anxiously.

In the midst of all the excitement Miss Evans came over to Andrew and asked him to follow her to her room.

'I haven't decided what kind of costume to make for you, Andrew,' she said. 'I wondered about just giving you a puppet of a golden bird to hold. It might be the easiest.'

Andrew looked alarmed. He wouldn't be able to move his wings if he was holding a puppet.

'Or I could make you a gold costume and fasten some stiff wings to the back. They're rather heavy so you'd have to stand very still, but you wouldn't mind that, would you?'

He bowed his head, and Miss Evans sighed. She might as well be talking to herself.

'You only have to stand behind the Sleeping Beauty while everyone sings your golden bird song, don't you? It's not as if you're expected to do anything, Andrew. We just want you to look good.'

Andrew waited until he was quite sure that Miss Evans didn't have anything else to say to him. Then, when she was looking through her pile of materials, he slipped out of her room. She looked up, holding some wire that she thought of twisting into a beak for him, and sighed again.

After the rehearsal had finished, Mr Swain packed away all the costumes in the wicker basket and wheeled them back to Miss Evans' room. He realised he had forgotten the cook's floppy hat and went back to fetch it. Andrew was alone in the hall. He was standing with his back to him. He didn't hear Mr Swain come in. Mr Swain backed out again silently and hurried down to Miss Evans' room.

'Come quickly,' he said. 'I think we've solved the problem of the golden bird's costume.'

They crept to the doorway of the hall and peeped in, hardly daring to breathe in case Andrew saw them. There he was, moving slowly and gracefully up and down the hall. His head was cocked to one side, his eyes

were bright and shining, and his wings
were rippling for flight.

Four

AT LAST THE day of the performance
came. It was to be held in the evening,
and the day seemed to last for ever.
The only thing the children wanted to
think about was the play. They argued
about who had the most people coming
to see it.

'I've got the most,' said Shaz. 'My
mum's bringing all her circus class
friends – so you'd better be good!' she
warned the jugglers.

'All my aunties are coming,' said Lynne. 'And I've got nine!'

Andrew was the only one who didn't join in the general chatter. He hadn't even mentioned the play to his mother. He hardly talked, even at home, since the day he had started to be unhappy.

That was the day his father had died.

He wished he could have told his father about the golden bird. But he couldn't tell his mother. She was too busy, too tired, too sad.

On the morning of the play, Andrew's mother went down to the school. She waited for Mr Swain to park his motorbike and take off his crash helmet, and then she went up to him. She could see Andrew sitting all by himself in the yard, while a group of children swept past him. Suddenly he spread his arms out and wheeled round, then just as suddenly he stood still again, as if he knew he was being watched.

'Could I have a word with you, Mr Swain. I'm worried about Andrew,' she said. 'Just look at him! He's doing that kind of thing all the time at home, pecking and bobbing his head, moving his arms up and down every time he thinks I'm not watching. Do you know – he seems to think he's a bird!'

To her surprise, Mr Swain only
laughed. 'It's all right,' he told her.
'He's only practising for the school
play. Didn't you know about it?!'

Andrew's mother shook her head.
'He never tells me anything.'

'Come and see it tonight,' Mr Swain
said. 'I think you'll enjoy it!'

Andrew's mother looked across at
her son as he bobbed his golden head
from side to side. 'I think I will,' she
said.

That afternoon the final rehearsal was held. For the very first time the children rehearsed in their costumes. Everything went wrong. The jugglers dropped their juggling balls, the fairies got the giggles, the king forgot two of his speeches, Sleeping Beauty had hiccoughs when she was supposed to be in a deep sleep. And when Andrew's moment came to stand behind her and spread out his wings as if he was going to fly off in search of the prince, he found he couldn't move. He couldn't lift his arms up, or turn his head, or bend his knees, or anything. He was frozen with fright.

'What use is that golden bird?' said Lynne as they were all hanging up their costumes. 'He might just as well be a stick insect!'

Five

AT SEVEN O'CLOCK the children could
hear the buzz of the audience as the
school hall began to fill up. They stood,
nervous and excited, behind the curtain,
waiting for the moment when Mr
Swain would lift his hand and the
musicians would start to play. They
were all anxious because of the mistakes
they had made at the dress rehearsal,
but Mr Swain promised them that
everything would be all right.

'You'll be wonderful,' he said. 'Enjoy it!' He lifted up his hand, and they were on!

Andrew had to wait a long time before his turn came to go on stage. He felt his stomach growing cold inside him. He felt sick and trembling. The music and the laughter, the singing and the applause, swirled round him in waves. He wanted to go home. He wanted to crawl into the quiet darkness of his bed and never come out again.

Then at last he felt Mr Swain's hand on his shoulder.

'Now, Andrew!'

He heard the children singing on stage,

'Golden bird, keep her safe,
Golden bird, keep her safe,
Guard her from all harm.'

He stepped onto the stage. The lights dazzled him. He paused for a moment, then tried to remember exactly what he had seen when he had watched the birds playing in the yard.

He bent his knees a little, so his back
could curve over. He stretched out his
neck. He peered straight down his
nose, and cocked his head in little jerks
and bobs from side to side. He forgot
everything except the little bird-like
movements he was making.

Now he could feel a hush descending
on the room. The Sleeping Beauty and
the king and queen and all the
courtiers were asleep, and only he
could save them. He flexed his

shoulder blades. That was where his
wings started from. He bent his elbows
into his sides then slowly, slowly, lifted
them up and stretched out his arms as
far as they would go. There was a gasp
from the audience. His golden feathers
fluttered up around him as he lifted his
wings above his head. He rose on his
feet and crouched down again, rose
again, then stroked the air with his
wings.

Again and again he lifted himself up, and at last he felt the air turn below him. He tucked his legs in and away out again as if he was swimming, and he thrust his wings slowly down and up, down and up, down and up. Far below him he could see the people of the audience, their faces upturned and their mouths round holes of astonishment and joy. He could feel the air rushing past him like water, he could hear it whispering through his feathers. He could see around him all the lights of the stars in the night sky, and his wings gleamed gold in the moonlight.

Six

'YOU WERE BRILLIANT!' Lynne shouted. 'I don't know how you did that! You were brilliant!'

Andrew gazed round him. He was standing in the middle of the stage, and the audience were cheering and clapping and shouting. He had to go forward again and again to bow to them.

And when the curtain came down at last the king and queen and Sleeping Beauty and the prince and the cook and all the fairies were patting his shoulders and congratulating him. Mr Swain was beaming at him.

And then he saw his mother. She was full of smiles, just as she used to be. She knelt down and hugged him.

'I wish your dad could have seen you!' she said.

'So do I,' said Andrew. 'But I'm glad you came, Mum.'

He looked round at Mr Swain, and at all the smiling friends, and he knew that he was happy again.